C901699861

D0618932

DISCARDED

Special thanks to Linda Chapman
To Eve and Rose Williams, the most
wonderful daughters anyone could wish for!

ORCHARD BOOKS

First published in Great Britain in 2016 by The Watts Publishing Group

1 3 5 7 9 10 8 6 4 2

Text copyright © Hothouse Fiction, 2016
Illustrations copyright © Orchard Books, 2016

The moral rights of the author and illustrator have been asserted.

All characters and events in this publication, other than those clearly in the public domain, are fictitious and any resemblance to real persons, living or dead, is purely coincidental.

All rights reserved.
No part of this publication may be reproduced, stored in a retrieval system, or transmitted, in any form or by any means, without the prior permission in writing of the publisher, nor be otherwise circulated in any form of binding or cover other than that in which it is published and without a similar condition including this condition being imposed on the subsequent purchaser.

A CIP catalogue record for this book
is available from the British Library.

ISBN 978 1 40833 608 3

Printed and bound in Great Britain by Clays Ltd, St Ives plc

The paper and board used in this book are made from wood from responsible sources.

Orchard Books
An imprint of
Hachette Children's Group
Part of The Watts Publishing Group Limited
Carmelite House
50 Victoria Embankment
London EC4Y 0DZ

An Hachette UK Company
www.hachette.co.uk
www.hachettechildrens.co.uk

Series created by Hothouse Fiction
www.hothousefiction.com

Secret PRINCESSES

The Magic
Necklace

ROSIE BANKS

Wishing Star Palace

The Secret Princess Promise

"I promise that I will be kind and brave,

Using my magic to help and save,

Granting wishes and doing my best,

To make people smile and bring happiness."

# CONTENTS

CHAPTER ONE
Important News

"Reach to the sky, don't look down. Life's a dance, so smile don't frown!" Charlotte Williams sang the words of her favourite song while she and her best friend, Mia Thompson, danced around her bedroom. When the music reached the final chorus, they let go of each other's hands. As Mia watched, Charlotte did a kick and then

shook her hips like Alice De Silver, the pop
star who sang the song. Charlotte tried to do
a cartwheel but there wasn't enough space in
her small bedroom so she finished by sliding
into the splits, holding her arms up high as
the music ended.

Mia clapped, then collapsed on to Charlotte's bed, her long blonde hair fanning out behind her on the pink duvet.

Charlotte grinned. "That was fun! Let's play that song again."

"I'm puffed out!" panted Mia.

"No, you're not." Charlotte bounced on to the bed beside her. She pulled at Mia's hands. "Come on! Dance with me. Pleeease!" She widened her brown eyes.

Mia grinned and let herself be pulled up. "OK! As long as the routine isn't too tricky."

"Cool! We could show it to our mums after we've worked it out," Charlotte said. Both their mums were downstairs drinking tea. They were good friends, too.

"No way!" exclaimed Mia. Unlike Charlotte, Mia was shy and hated being the centre of attention. "I'm not a brilliant dancer like you."

"You are!" Charlotte insisted. "But how about we just pretend there's an audience. We could be Alice De Silver's backing dancers!"

Mia was happy to do that! She had a big imagination and loved making up stories almost as much as she loved reading them.

Mia and Charlotte had known each other ever since they were babies. When the girls had been two, they had started at the local playgroup together and after that they had gone to the same school. Even though they

were opposites in lots of ways, Charlotte and
Mia were best friends.

Charlotte did a handstand against the
wall, the ends of her brown
curls touching the floor.

Mia picked up the
CD case and looked
at the girl on the
cover. Alice De Silver
had shoulder-length,
wavy, strawberry-
blonde hair
with cool red
streaks. In
the photo on the
cover she was

wearing a short silver skirt, silver platform shoes and a red crop top. The album was called *Pop Princess*. "I still can't believe we know a real live pop star," she said dreamily.

Charlotte dropped her legs to the ground
and stood up. "I know," she agreed. "It's so
weird to think that Alice used to babysit us,
isn't it?"

Mia nodded. "I really miss her."

"Me, too," said Charlotte.

Alice's parents lived next door to
Charlotte. Alice was eighteen and loved
singing. A year ago, when she was still plain
old Alice Silver, she'd won a TV talent
competition and become a pop star. Her
first song, 'Friendship Is Forever', had been
a huge hit all over the world. She lived
in London now and the girls didn't see her
much, although she sometimes sent them
tickets for her concerts. She had always been

like a big sister to them. The coolest big sister in the world!

"Maybe if we work out a really good routine we could video it and send it to her," Charlotte said. "I bet she'd like to see it."

Mia pulled a funny face. "I've got an even better idea," she said. "*You* dance and I'll video you!"

"OK, but you have to help me work out what to do." Charlotte turned the music on again. "Come on!"

They were just working out the opening steps when Charlotte's mum came into the bedroom. She was carrying a tray with a plate full of biscuits and two cartons of apple juice.

"Hi, girls. I thought you might like a drink to go with the cookies that Mia made us. They're really delicious, Mia."

"Thanks," Mia said shyly. She loved making things for her friends and family.

"Yum," said Charlotte, taking a bite. "These are amazing!"

Her mum smiled. "You haven't got much longer, I'm afraid. Mia and her mum are going home soon."

"Awwwww," said Charlotte. She gave her

mum a hopeful look. "Can Mia sleep over?"

"Not tonight, sweetheart," her mum said. "Dad's coming home early. We've got some news to talk to you and your brothers about."

"What news?" Charlotte asked curiously.

Her mum smiled, her cheeks dimpling just like Charlotte's did. "It's a surprise."

Charlotte gave Mia a puzzled look as her mum left the room. "I wonder what it is?"

"Maybe you're getting a pet?" said Mia. She and her little sister had a cat, two guinea pigs and lots of fish – but she really wanted to get a dog. For her, that would be the best surprise ever.

Charlotte shook her head. "I doubt it. The twins are allergic to animals."

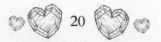

"Oh, yeah," Mia said, with a sigh. She helped herself to a biscuit and grinned. "Maybe Alice sent your family tickets to her next show."

"That would be cool," Charlotte said. Grinning, she added, "But not as cool as being on stage myself!" She jumped to her feet, turned the music up and dragged Mia up to perform their dance routine again.

The girls danced until the song ended and then landed in a giggly heap on the bed.

"Mia! It's time to go home!" Mia's mum called up the stairs.

They went downstairs. Charlotte gave Mia a hug goodbye and then went through to the kitchen. "So, what's the big news, Mum?" she asked.

"I'll tell you later when we're all together. Can you help me set the table for supper? Dad's bringing pizza home."

"Yay!" Pizza was Charlotte's favourite food. She started to get the plates out. "Is it about a holiday?"

"Not telling," her mum said. Her eyes sparkled. "But it *is* something exciting."

"Is it something to do with that job interview you had the other day?" Charlotte guessed.

"It might be, but you'll just have to be patient," her mum said.

Charlotte sighed. She hated being patient but she had no choice, as her mum refused to say anything more.

At last Dad arrived home with two large cardboard boxes filled with takeaway pizza. Charlotte went to fetch her twin six-year-old brothers, Liam and Harvey, who were playing computer games, as usual.

"We need to finish this game," said Liam. Charlotte's brothers looked just like her, with curly hair and dark skin. Liam had longer

hair and Harvey's was very short – and
sometimes that was the only way Charlotte
could tell them apart!

"Yeah, we've nearly made it to the next
level!" said Harvey.

"OK, but there's takeaway pizza," said
Charlotte. "And if you don't come soon, I'll
eat it all!"

"Pizza!" The two boys threw their game
controllers down and raced to the kitchen.

"Tuck in, everyone," Dad said, as they all
sat down.

Charlotte took a slice of pepperoni pizza.
The cheese was all stringy just as she liked it.
"So, come on, Mum," she said impatiently.
"What's the news?"

Her mum took a deep breath and grinned. "Well, I have something really exciting to tell you all. I've been offered a new job and guess what?" She paused with a huge smile. "It's not in England, it's in California. We're moving to America in six weeks' time!"

CHAPTER TWO
Best Friends For Ever

Charlotte stared at her mum. They were moving to América! But that would mean leaving school, leaving their house – and, worst of all, leaving Mia!

"America! Cool!" said Liam.

"Awesome!" said Harvey. "We can play baseball! And American football!"

"Isn't California by the sea?" Liam said.

Their dad nodded. "It's really sunny there. You'll be able to learn how to surf."

The twins whooped and high-fived each other. "This is mega!" said Liam.

Charlotte put her pizza down on her plate. Suddenly, she didn't feel hungry at all. She couldn't believe that her little brothers were so happy. Then again, they were twins – not just brothers, but best friends too. But *her* best friend couldn't come with her.

Her mum glanced at her. "Are you OK, Charlotte?"

Charlotte could feel tears in her eyes but she bravely fought them back.

"It'll be a really fun adventure," her mum told her. "We're going to rent a big house.

You'll have a much larger bedroom and there'll be a big garden too."

"Or 'yard', as the Americans call it," said her dad. "You'll be able to play outside all the time because the weather's much better there – you can even go to the beach every day if you want. Don't you think it sounds amazing?"

There was a hard lump in Charlotte's throat. She had to force her words past it. "I'll miss Mia."

Her mum and dad exchanged looks.

"Oh, sweetheart," Mum said, taking her hand. "You and Mia will be able to keep in touch. You can Skype each other and email, and in the holidays she can come and visit."

"It won't be the same," Charlotte said.

"You'll make new friends over there," her dad reassured her.

"But they won't be Mia." A tear rolled down Charlotte's cheek. Mia wasn't just a friend, she was her best friend, and best friends were for ever. They couldn't just be replaced like a pair of jeans. Charlotte's heart twisted as she thought about telling Mia the news. She knew most people would think she was really lucky, but she just couldn't imagine life without Mia.

The next six weeks flew by. The day before
Charlotte and her family were due to leave
for America, Mia's parents held a huge
leaving party for them. It was a barbecue
with a Californian theme. Everyone
had come dressed in surfing clothes and
sundresses, even though it was grey and
cloudy outside. Charlotte and Mia helped

to carry bowls of salad and crisps out to the garden. Harvey and Liam's friends were jumping round to the music and kicking a football on the lawn, while the adults stood around talking and laughing.

"Come on, girls! Let's dance!" called Mia's dad as he jigged around holding a jug of fruit punch covered in paper umbrellas.

"Maybe later, Dad," said Charlotte quietly. For the first time ever she didn't feel like dancing.

"Should we go up to my room?" Mia whispered.

Charlotte nodded sadly. They were both wearing bright sundresses, but their moods were gloomy.

They went upstairs. Mia's room had
posters of kittens, horses and puppies on the
walls. Animal stories and pretty things that
she'd made filled her bookshelves. There was
pretty lilac bunting looped over her bed and
she had a matching lilac duvet with cats on
it. Charlotte sighed as she thought of all the
fun sleepovers they'd had.

"I've got a present for you," said Mia.
Charlotte sat down on the bed while Mia got

a large scrapbook, then sat beside her. The
scrapbook had a pink cover and '*Best Friends
Are Forever*' was written in glitter on the
front. "I made this for you," Mia said. "I hope
you like it."

Charlotte opened it. It was full of photos
of them both. They started when they
were babies lying on a playmat together,
then when they were toddlers dressed as
princesses, and then on their first day at
school when they were wearing uniforms that
looked much too big and both had their hair
in sticking-out bunches.

"Oh, wow," she said, turning the pages.
"This is awesome. I love it!" Mia had also
stuck in some special things amongst the

photos – a birthday card Charlotte had sent
her when she was five, a rule book from the
friendship club they had made up together,
and a ticket stub from Alice's first concert
that they had gone to last year. Charlotte
bit her lip, feeling happy and sad at the same
time. "Thank you. I'll keep it for ever."

"Which is how long we'll be friends for,"
said Mia.

They hugged each other. "I don't want to
go," whispered Charlotte, her eyes stinging
with tears.

"I don't want you to, either," said Mia
bravely. "But we'll always be best friends.
No matter how far apart we are."

"Always," promised Charlotte.

As they hugged, there was a knock at the door. The girls looked at each other in surprise.

"Come in!" called Mia. A beautiful older girl with strawberry-blonde hair streaked with bright red opened the door. She was wearing a short denim skirt and sparkly sandals. On her white top rested the necklace she always wore, a gold pendant shaped like a musical note, so shiny that it almost seemed to glow.

"Alice!" Charlotte and Mia gasped, jumping to their feet.

Their pop star friend looked incredibly glamorous, but her smile was just as warm as ever. "Your mums are looking for you.

I thought I might find you up here."

They ran over and hugged her. "How come you're back?" Mia said.

"Your mum emailed me about the party and I really wanted to come. I'm only here for a few hours, though. I have to travel up north for a concert I'm doing tomorrow night, but I just couldn't let Charlotte go to California without saying goodbye," Alice said.

"I can't believe you're moving."

"I know," said Charlotte.

They all sat down on the bed together. Despite feeling miserable about leaving, Charlotte couldn't help but smile as she looked at Alice. It was so nice to see her again. "I'm so glad you could come."

Alice squeezed her hand. "So why aren't you two downstairs dancing?"

Mia swallowed. "We didn't feel like it."

Alice's blue eyes softened. "I know it's hard, but you can still be best friends even if you're far apart."

"It's just not going to be the same," said Charlotte, sighing. "We won't be able to see each other much at all."

Best Friends For Ever

Alice looked from one girl to the other.
"Maybe you will."

"What do you mean?" asked Charlotte
in surprise.

Alice smiled mysteriously and pulled
something out of her pocket. It was a
golden necklace. "Charlotte and Mia,"
she murmured. She closed her hand for a

moment and waved
her other hand
over it.

When Alice
opened her hand
again, there
were two
necklaces
nestled in
her palm!

"How ... how did you do that?" stammered
Mia, astonished.

Alice jumped to her feet. "There isn't time
to explain right now. Just remember this ..."
She handed them each a necklace. "Wishes
do come true. As long as you keep each other

in your hearts, you'll never be alone. Now quick – put the necklaces on!"

Charlotte fastened the necklace she was holding around Mia's neck, then Mia did the same for her. As soon as the necklaces were around their necks there was a tinkling sound and a bright flash of light.

"Oh my gosh!" said Charlotte. A pendant in the shape of half a heart had appeared on Mia's necklace. Charlotte looked down and gasped. Hanging from her own necklace was a pendant just like Mia's!

Mia's eyes were wide as she stared in amazement. "But ... but that's impossible!" she whispered as she looked at the beautiful half-heart pendant.

"Not impossible – magic!" Alice said softly, before hugging them both. "I knew you two were special!" she said mysteriously.

Mia gently lifted her pendant and held it against Charlotte's. Together, they formed a perfect heart. Mia's hand tingled as the heart began to glow, filling her bedroom with warm, bright light. She was so excited she could barely breathe.

"Charlotte! Mia! Come down or you'll miss the whole party!" Charlotte's mum called from downstairs, breaking the spell. Startled, the girls dropped their pendants and they stopped glowing.

The girls looked at each other in amazement. But before they could ask Alice

any questions, she grabbed their hands and smiled. "Come on, let's dance together while we still have a chance!" And with that, they all ran downstairs.

CHAPTER THREE
Sunny California

A week later, Charlotte and her family were eating breakfast in their new kitchen.

"I love American breakfasts!" Liam said, squeezing maple syrup onto a huge pile of fluffy pancakes.

"Me, too," Harvey agreed, through a mouthful of bacon.

The twins and Charlotte were sitting at

the breakfast bar while their mum cooked pancakes and their dad squeezed fresh orange juice from oranges that he had just picked in their garden. There were still boxes everywhere. To Charlotte it still felt like they were on holiday in California rather than living in their own house. Everything seemed so different.

"Can I have another pancake, Mum?" asked Harvey.

"Here you go," said their mum, bringing a pile of pancakes over to the table.

Even the pancakes are different in America, Charlotte thought. They were thick and round, not at all like the thin pancakes they ate in England. Still, they were very nice. She helped herself to another one and poured some yummy sweet syrup on.

"So, what does everyone want to do today?" her dad asked.

Her mum joined the rest of the family at the table. "I think I'm going to spend the day doing some more unpacking."

"I want to finish my room," said Charlotte.

She'd started at her new school a few days after they had arrived and she hadn't had a chance to unpack all her things yet.

"Boring!" said Liam. "I want to go to the beach."

"Me, too," said Harvey. "Brad and Ty from school asked if we wanted to play beach volleyball. Can you take us, Dad?"

"Sure," Dad replied. "Are you sure you don't want to come with us, Charlotte?"

"I'm good, thanks," said Charlotte.

Her mum smiled. "You're already starting to sound American."

"No one at school thinks so," said Charlotte. "They keep asking me to say things because they like my accent."

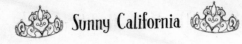

"How's school going?" her dad asked.

"OK," said Charlotte, shrugging. "But it's weird calling things by different names. Breaktime is called 'recess' here."

"And rubbers are 'erasers'," Harvey added.

Most of the girls and boys in Charlotte's class had been really friendly and she liked her teacher, Ms Impey. Instead of being in year four she was now in third grade. On the first day she had found it strange to go to school wearing shorts and a T-shirt rather than a school uniform, but it was fun being able to choose what to wear each day. They did lots of sports at school and she'd already joined the gymnastics club and softball team. There was only one thing missing – Mia.

Thinking about Mia made Charlotte's heart ache. She hadn't forgotten Alice's words about staying best friends, but it hadn't stopped her from missing Mia a lot. She glanced down at her necklace. She wasn't sure how Alice had done the clever trick with the necklaces, but she wished that they really were magic. Then she could magic herself back together with Mia.

"Isn't there a school dance tonight for third and fourth graders?" asked her mum.

"Yeah," said Charlotte.

"I thought so. It sounds like fun."

"I'm not going, Mum," said Charlotte. Two nice girls from her class, Ava and Leah, had asked her yesterday if she wanted to

go with them, but she'd said no.

"Why?" her mum said. "You love dancing."

"I just don't want to," said Charlotte.

She finished her pancakes and cleared away her plate, then went upstairs to her new bedroom. It was much bigger than her old room. It had a wooden floor, cream walls and a view of the orange trees in the garden.

There was even a built-in wardrobe for all her clothes. No, not wardrobe, Charlotte remembered as she flopped down on her bed. Here it was called a closet. That was one more difference. She felt a wave of homesickness.

Charlotte sat up on her bed and wondered what Mia was doing now. It was nine o'clock in the morning here in California, so it was five o'clock in the afternoon in the UK. If she still lived there, she'd probably be going to Mia's house for a Saturday-night sleepover.

Charlotte touched the half-heart pendant on her necklace. "Oh, Mia," she whispered. "I wish I could be with you right now."

Her fingers tingled as if an electric current

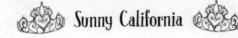

was running through the
necklace. She pulled her
hand back in surprise.
What was happening?

Glancing down,
Charlotte saw that
the necklace had
begun to glow.
The warm light
radiated out and
surrounded
Charlotte, like
someone was
shining a
spotlight
on her.

Blinking in shock, Charlotte suddenly felt herself being swept away and leaving her bedroom behind …

Excitement rushed through her. *It is magic, after all!* Charlotte thought. Finally, she felt her feet touch the ground again.

As the bright light started to fade, she blinked and looked around. She was in a beautiful garden. But there was something strange about it – the garden was surrounded by wispy white puffs. Charlotte peered at them more closely and suddenly realised

what they were – clouds! The whole garden was floating in the sky!

"Oh, wow!" she breathed. "Where am I?" The garden had a lush green lawn with paths leading around flowers beds that were overflowing with pink, blue and lilac flowers. Trees dotted the lawn, some with silver branches covered with fluffy pastel-coloured blossom and others with big, round

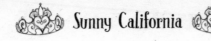
lollipops hanging from the
branches on silver sticks.
Charlotte couldn't believe
her eyes.

She hurried towards the
nearest lollipop tree to
take a closer look.

"Charlotte!"

Charlotte swung round.
Mia was standing behind
her on one of the paths.

"Mia!" Charlotte gasped
out loud.

They ran to each other
and hugged, squealing
with delight.

"What's going on?" Mia asked. "I was reading in my bedroom when suddenly my necklace started glowing, and everything went all bright and swirly. When I opened my eyes I was here!"

"I wished I could see you!" said Charlotte. "Our necklaces really are magic!"

They both glanced down at their necklaces. Their half-heart pendants were still glowing.

"This is so amazing!" Charlotte shrieked, throwing her arms around Mia again. The girls squeezed each other tightly, and Charlotte felt happiness rush through her. There was just nothing like being with her very best friend!

Finally, the girls broke apart and looked around in excitement.

"Have you seen what's growing on the trees?" Charlotte said. Grabbing Mia's hand, they went and sat under the lollipop tree.

"And look – that one's got candyfloss on it!" said Mia, pointing at the next tree.

Charlotte realised that the tree's branches weren't covered with blossom, but with pink and blue candyfloss!

"Do you think we can taste it?" Charlotte asked excitedly.

"You should – it's delicious," said a familiar voice. Mia and Charlotte swung round to find Alice standing behind them! But she wasn't wearing her pop-star clothes. She was wearing a red princess gown with a full skirt and beaded bodice. There was a diamond-studded tiara in her strawberry-blonde hair and she was wearing sparkling red shoes. In one hand she held a slim, silver wand. The musical note on the end of it matched the pendant on her necklace.

"Alice?" Charlotte said in astonishment, wondering if she was dreaming.

Alice grinned. "Surprise!" She hurried over and hugged them both. "It's lovely to see you two here. Welcome to Wishing Star Palace!"

CHAPTER FOUR
Wishing Star Palace

"Did she say palace?" Charlotte whispered to Mia. The girls swapped mystified looks as Alice led the way down a path. As they turned a corner, the girls gasped. A white palace rose up in front of them, its four pointed turrets silhouetted against the blue sky. The windows were heart-shaped, and pink and red roses climbed up the walls.

At the top of
each turret flew
a pretty purple flag
with a sparkling tiara on it.

"Oh, my!" whispered Mia breathlessly.

"This is Wishing Star Palace," said Alice.
"It's where all the Secret Princesses come
and meet."

"Secret Princesses?" echoed Charlotte. "What are they?"

"Secret Princesses are special people who grant wishes to make other people happy," said Alice. "I'm one of them. We all share certain qualities, like kindness, creativity and

bravery, but we each have our own special talents too."

The girls looked at her, feeling totally confused. Charlotte put her hand in Mia's. No matter what was going on, if she got to see her best friend she was happy!

Alice smiled. "I know it's a lot to take in. Why don't you come and meet some of the other Secret Princesses and then you'll see what I mean? But first I think you need a change of clothes – something more princessy would be good." She lifted her wand and called out a spell:

"Clothes transform into dresses fine,
Sparkle and glow, shimmer and shine!"

There was a bright flash and Charlotte and Mia's everyday clothes changed into princess dresses just like Alice's. Charlotte's was a light pink with gorgeous pink roses on the skirt. Mia's dress was gold with sparkly sequins around the bottom and a big bow around her waist. On top of their heads they each wore a delicate gold tiara.

"Oh, wow, wow, wow!" said Charlotte, twirling around in delight.

"This is the most beautiful dress ever," said Mia, stroking the skirt as if she could hardly dare to believe she was wearing it.

"Good," said Alice, with a smile. "Now, why don't we go inside."

They walked over the long bridge up

to the big front door.

As the girls got nearer to the palace, Charlotte frowned slightly. Now she was closer, she could see that the palace was actually quite shabby.

Some of the panes of glass in the doors and windows were cracked, the white paint under the roses was peeling and coming away from the walls, the doors were hanging at a slightly odd angle and there were tiles missing from one of the turrets.

Alice sighed. "I'm sorry that you have to see the palace like this. It used to be so beautiful. Look!"

She waved her wand. The air shimmered and, for a few seconds, the palace was transformed. Its white walls glowed and sparkled like freshly fallen snow, the panes of glass glittered like diamonds, the window ledges were made of shining gold and the turrets weren't missing any tiles.

The image faded and the palace returned to the crumbling reality. Compared to the gorgeous palace Alice had showed them, it looked even shabbier than before.

"What happened?" asked Mia.

But before Alice could answer, another princess came out of the doors and stood on the top of the steps. She had deep red hair that was piled into a bun, with ringlets escaping down her cheeks. She was wearing a dark green dress and had a gold necklace with a cupcake pendant. She waved. "Hello! You must be Mia and Charlotte!"

"Yes," said Charlotte in surprise, wondering how she knew their names.

"I'm Princess Sylvie," said the princess.

"Do you like cupcakes? I've just baked a fresh batch. They're still warm!"

"Yum!" said Alice. "Sylvie's cupcakes are the best ever," she told the girls.

"I'll go and get them," said Princess Sylvie.

Alice and the girls walked through the doors and into a huge room with large windows and comfy chairs. There were two

other princesses inside. One was standing
at an easel, painting a portrait of the other
princess who was sitting in a chair, cuddling
a fluffy white kitten. The princess who was
painting had olive skin and long brown
hair that fell almost to her waist. She was
wearing a sunshine-yellow dress and her
pendant was shaped like a paintbrush.

"Aw, sweet!" cooed Mia, longing to give the kitten a cuddle.

"Hello, Mia! Hello, Charlotte!" said the princess being painted, waving at the girls. She had short black hair and smiling, almond-shaped brown eyes. She was wearing a light blue dress and had a paw-shaped pendant. "I'm Princess Ella."

"And I'm Princess Sophie," said the other princess, smiling.

"Alice has told us all about you two," said Princess Ella.

The picture on the easel waved.

"We're all so thrilled you've finally arrived!" said the painting of Princess Ella in a tiny, tinkly voice.

The girls stared in amazement.

"Er – the picture's talking to us," said Mia with a gasp.

"Yes, you'll see all sorts of wonderful, magical things here," said Alice, with a chuckle. "Everyone is so excited to see you."

"But why?" Charlotte burst out.

"Because we think you might be able to help us," Alice said. She took Mia and Charlotte's hands. "We think you two might be able to save Wishing Star Palace!"

Charlotte and Mia stared at Alice.

"You think *we* can help save the palace?"

Charlotte's mind spun. How could she and Mia possibly do that?

"But … but how? We're not magic," said Mia, clearly thinking the same thing. "We're just ordinary girls."

Alice laughed. "Every one of us Secret Princesses was once just an ordinary girl, too. But we all have a special gift – for baking or painting, or music."

"We keep our magic a secret," Princess Sophie chimed in. "All of us have other jobs in the real world. I'm an artist, Ella's a vet and Sylvie runs a cake shop."

"And Alice is a singer," Charlotte said.

"That's right," said Alice. "We use our special talents to help people." Giving the

kitten on Ella's lap a pat, she added, "Or, in Ella's case, animals."

"Is that why you've got a paw-print pendant on your necklace?" Mia asked Princess Ella, with a shy smile.

Princes Ella nodded. "Exactly! Your necklace shows what your special talent is."

"Cupcake time!" Princess Sylvie came into the room with a silver tray piled high with delicious-looking cupcakes, covered with swirly buttercream.

"Cupcakes first, then I'll explain," Alice promised the girls. Charlotte was about to take one when Princess Sylvie swooped over and stopped them. "Wait! You have to choose what flavour you want first."

"But aren't they all the same?" said Charlotte, feeling puzzled. All the cupcakes looked identical.

"What's your favourite flavour?" Princess Sylvie asked.

"Chocolate," said Charlotte instantly, imagining a gooey chocolate cupcake.

Mia thought for a moment. "I like raspberry and white chocolate," she said.

Sylvie smiled at them and waved her wand. Silver sparkles appeared and sprinkled

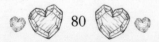

onto the icing. All of a sudden, Charlotte's
cake was covered with thick swirls of
chocolate and little silver stars, while Mia's
cupcake had pink icing with white chocolate
sprinkles and a lovely, plump raspberry in
the middle.

Sylvie beamed. "Now try them."

Charlotte bit into her cupcake and closed
her eyes. "Mmmmmmmm!" she sighed as

her mouth filled with the taste of rich milk chocolate. "It's delicious."

"So's mine," said Mia, licking her lips.

Alice grinned. "I told you Sylvie's cupcakes are the best."

As they ate, Charlotte said, "Mia is really good at baking, too. I'm surprised her necklace doesn't have a cupcake pendant – or a biscuit!"

"And yours should have a ballet shoe," Mia said, smiling at her friend.

"You both have lots of talents," Alice said. "But your pendants are special. Matching half-heart pendants are very, very rare."

Charlotte and Mia glanced down at their necklaces in surprise.

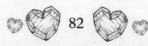

"You both share the most important Secret Princess quality," continued Alice.

The girls exchanged a puzzled look, trying to guess what Alice meant.

"Friendship!" all of the Secret Princesses said together.

"But lots of girls have a best friend," said Mia, fiddling with her heart pendant.

"True," said Alice, "but it's very rare to find two friends who *both* have Secret Princess qualities, and a friendship strong enough to weather any storm. Your necklaces show that you both have the potential to be Friendship Princesses."

Mia reached for Charlotte's hand and gave it an excited squeeze.

"Friendship Princesses always come in pairs," explained Princess Sophie. "The last two lived a hundred years ago." She waved her wand and an old book magically

appeared on her lap. She leafed through
it and showed the girls an old black and
white picture of two girls. Their heads were
touching and around their necks they had
matching half-heart pendants, just like
Charlotte's and Mia's.

"There haven't been any other Friendship
Princesses since Florence and Esme," said
Alice. "Until now ..." She
looked at Charlotte's
and Mia's pendants.

"But we're not Secret
Princesses," said Mia.
"I mean ...
we can't do
magic."

"Not yet," said Alice. "But if you train to be Secret Princesses, you'll learn how."

Mia gripped Charlotte's hand even more tightly, and bit her lip to stop herself from squealing with excitement.

"And if you do well and complete your training, you'll become proper Secret Princesses," continued Alice.

"With lots more magical powers," said Sylvie. She twirled around and her green dress spun out, changing to a different colour with every turn.

"Yippee!" cried Charlotte. She might become a Secret Princess – and, best of all, she could do it with her very best friend!

"What do we have to do?" asked Mia, slightly nervously.

"You'll work together to help make people happy by granting wishes," said Alice.

Mia gasped in delight.

"So, what do you think?" asked Alice.

"Would you like to become trainee Secret Princesses?"

Charlotte and Mia didn't need to think twice. "Yes, please!" they chorused.

CHAPTER FIVE
The Magic Mirror

Alice hugged them. "That's wonderful!
Ever since you were little, I suspected you
two might have the potential to be Secret
Princesses, but I never dreamed you'd be
Friendship Princesses. I was so excited when
I saw the two half-heart pendants appear!
With your help, we might be able to save
Wishing Star Palace."

"So, why is it falling down?" asked
Charlotte. "What's happened to it?"

"Because of Princess Poison," Alice told
them grimly.

The other three princesses all shivered.

Charlotte glanced at Mia. Princess Poison!
The name alone was scary. If this princess
was making the palace fall to bits then she
must be really horrible.

"Who ... who is Princess Poison?" Mia said
rather nervously.

"Come upstairs to the portrait gallery and
I'll explain," said Alice.

Waving goodbye to the other princesses,
Mia and Charlotte followed Alice out of
the sunny lounge and out into a hall with a

large winding
staircase
and wooden
floor. It had
obviously been
very grand at
one time, but
now the floor
was scuffed
and the paint
on the walls
was peeling.
Charlotte
longed to open
every single
door and go

and explore all the rooms leading off from
the hall, but Alice was already halfway up
the stairs.

"Here we are," Alice said, when they
reached the first floor landing. The walls on
both sides of the corridor were covered with
portraits of beautiful princesses. "This gallery
contains portraits of every Secret Princess,
past and present."

"Look – there's Princess Ella!" said Mia, inspecting one. "She's holding a puppy."

"And here you are, Alice!" said Charlotte, spotting a portrait of Alice singing into a microphone.

"Why is this one empty?" said Mia, looking at a frame with no picture inside.

"That was where Princess Poison's picture used to be," said Alice. She walked over to

 93

the frame and shook her head sadly. "She isn't a Secret Princess any more."

"Why not?" asked Mia, her eyes wide.

"Because she started using her magic to gain power for herself," said Alice. "Secret Princesses must never use their wishes selfishly. Princess Poison was banished from Wishing Star Palace for ever. Now she hates all the Secret Princesses. Every time she ruins one of our wishes she gets more powerful, and Wishing Star Palace crumbles a bit more."

"That's awful!" exclaimed Charlotte.

"I know. If we don't stop her, Wishing Star Palace will collapse. And without the magic of Wishing Star Palace, there won't be any more Secret Princesses!" Alice sobbed.

Tears welled in her
eyes and spilled over
her cheeks.

"How can we help?"
asked Mia. She hated
seeing Alice so sad.

"You already have
by agreeing to train as
Secret Princesses," said
Alice. "We desperately
need more trainee Secret Princesses to help
us grant wishes, but Princess Poison has been
causing trouble for them. She's very clever
and powerful, and most girls can't stand up
to her on their own. That's why we don't
have many new trainees at the moment.

But because you're Friendship Princesses, you two can work together – so hopefully you'll be able to stop Princess Poison if she does interfere."

"We'll do all we can to help!" declared Charlotte, holding Mia's hand and giving it a squeeze.

Mia nodded. Princess Poison sounded terrifying, but having Charlotte by her side made her feel brave. "We won't let Princess Poison stop us from granting wishes."

Alice smiled. "I knew we could count on you two!"

Suddenly, a light caught Charlotte's eye. The musical note on the end of Alice's wand had begun to glow.

"Your wand is shining, Alice!" Mia said.

"Oh, my goodness! When a Secret Princess's wand glows like that, it means someone needs our help. Usually one of us would go, but this could be your chance to start training. Are you ready?"

Charlotte and Mia looked at each other. "We are!" they said.

"Then follow me to the Mirror Room!" said Alice. "It's this way!"

Charlotte and Mia hurried along the corridor, past the Secret Princesses' portraits. Excitement fizzed through Charlotte. She and Mia were going to do magic!

At the end of the corridor there was a small spiral staircase that led up into a turret. They hurried up the stairs and came to a small door at the top. Alice opened it and they found themselves in a circular room. The only thing inside it was a large oval mirror on a tarnished gold stand. The surface of the glass was cloudy, but it swirled with silver and gold light.

"Touch the Magic Mirror," Alice said.

"It'll tell you what to do."

Charlotte and Mia reached out and touched their fingers to the shining surface of the mirror. Their fingers tingled as a bright flash ran across the surface, and then a rhyme appeared on the glass:

This is where
your journey starts.
Make four new friends
and heal their hearts.
Each wish you grant,
a diamond you will own.
Four will give you
your princess crown!

"So we need to grant four people's wishes," Mia said, checking that she'd understood the mirror's rhyme.

"That's right," said Alice. "On each of your adventures, you'll need to help one new friend. If you grant their wish, you'll earn a diamond. They'll be kept on your necklace for now."

Charlotte peered at her necklace. Now that she looked closely, she could see there was space for four gems on her pendant.

"Once you have all four jewels, you'll have passed your first part of princess training, and the diamonds will transform the plain training tiaras you're wearing now into full Secret Princess tiaras!" Alice pointed to

her own tiara, which shimmered with four diamonds. Then she touched her wand to the mirror's surface. The light started to swirl even faster, then suddenly it cleared, leaving the image of a girl a bit older than Charlotte and Mia. She was sitting on her bed, hugging her knees to her chest and looking very sad.

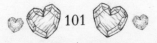

"The mirror shows us who needs help back in the real world," explained Alice.

"Olivia Simms," Charlotte said, reading out the name at the bottom of the glass.

"She looks worried," Mia said with concern.

"Look!" said Charlotte. A new rhyme had appeared on the mirror.

"A wish needs granting, adventures await,
Call Olivia's name, don't hesitate!"

"If you say Olivia's name together the mirror will take you both to her," said Alice.

"By magic?" guessed Mia.

"That's right," said Alice, nodding.

The girls grinned at each other, barely able to contain their excitement.

"But what about our parents?" asked Mia. "Won't they wonder where we are?"

"Don't worry," Alice reassured them. "No time passes in your real life when you're away making wishes come true. No one will even know you've been gone. So ... are you ready?"

Charlotte and Mia nodded eagerly.

"One, two, three ..." Alice looked at them expectantly.

"Olivia!" they cried together.

The light in the mirror started swirling again and the girls gasped as they felt themselves being gently pulled towards it.

Suddenly they were inside a swirling sea of light. Over and over they tumbled, getting faster and faster until they finally shot out and landed in a heap on a grassy lawn.

They sat up and looked around.

Mia was wearing a white party dress with lilac flowers embroidered on it. Charlotte's princess dress had changed into a floaty

turquoise skirt trimmed with sequins and a matching top.

"Where are we?" Mia whispered, looking around a front garden with neat flowerbeds full of white pansies.

"I guess this must be Olivia's house," Charlotte whispered back, looking at the large modern house in front of them.

The air beside them shimmered and, suddenly, Alice was standing there.

"How did you get here?" Charlotte asked in surprise.

Alice gave a laugh and pointed to her glittery red shoes.

"When you're fully-fledged Secret Princesses you can use your princess slippers to travel. One day you'll get some too, but for now, you can do magic by putting your necklaces together and making wishes. The necklaces will let you grant three wishes for each person," Alice continued, "but only while they're glowing. Once they stop glowing, the magic has run out."

"But why do we need three wishes? Can't we just make everything right with the first wish?" asked Charlotte.

"It's not that easy," Alice said, with a smile. "The magic in your necklaces can only grant small wishes. You can't just wish for someone's problems to be solved – you

have to think of little things that will help

them feel better. You need to use your three

wishes wisely. That's a Secret Princess's job!"

"Are you going to come with us?" asked

Mia anxiously.

"You must help Olivia on your own,"

replied Alice. "But I'll come back when

you've completed the task. Good luck!"

She stepped forward and kissed them both on the cheek. "Remember – always work together, never use wishes selfishly and keep a look out for Princess Poison."

"We will," Charlotte promised.

"Oh! And one last thing – you must keep your magic a secret. You can tell Olivia, but no one else, or the wish magic won't work."

"But won't other people notice what we've done?" wondered Mia.

"It's all part of the magic," Alice assured her. "You'll see."

She gave them one last smile, clicked her heels and vanished. Charlotte and Mia were on their own outside Olivia's house.

Just then the front door suddenly opened.

"Hello!" a lady called out.

Charlotte grabbed Mia's hand. "Here goes!" she whispered. "Let's make Olivia's wish come true!"

CHAPTER SIX
Olivia's Wish

"Are you here for the birthday party?" the lady called. Before Mia or Charlotte could reply, she carried on. "You're a bit early, but that's no problem. I'm sure Olivia will be happy to see you. Come in."

Charlotte and Mia exchanged quick looks but there didn't seem to be anything else they could do but go inside.

"I'm Olivia's mum, Joanne," said the lady.

"I'm Charlotte and this is Mia." Charlotte introduced them both.

"Pleased to meet you," Joanne said. "I guess you know Olivia from school." She ushered them into a large hallway. The walls were all painted white and the floor had glossy, black wooden boards. There was a large painting on one wall – bright splashes of colour on a white background. The house was more like an art gallery than a home. *The picture Princess Sophie was painting at Wishing Star Palace was much better,* Charlotte thought as they passed.

"Olivia!" Joanne called up the stairs. "Two of your guests have arrived early."

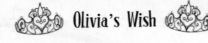

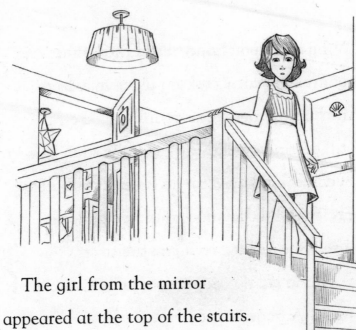

The girl from the mirror
appeared at the top of the stairs.
"Hi," she said, rather awkwardly.

"Well, I'd better go and get
myself ready," said Joanne.
"If you girls need anything just
ask Petra – she's our special
party planner," she explained
to Charlotte and Mia.

"Why don't you hang out in the living room? The party's taking place in a tent in the back garden," she continued. "Petra's still getting everything ready. We haven't even been allowed to see it yet. It's all very exciting. I'm sure it's going to be a lot of fun!" She hurried away up the stairs.

Olivia led the way into a large living room. A huge flat-screen TV was mounted on one wall and there was a fancy sound system with tall speakers, two big black leather sofas and a coffee table made completely of glass. Olivia gave them a curious look. "Did Petra invite you?"

"No," admitted Charlotte. "I'm Charlotte."

"And I'm Mia," said Mia shyly.

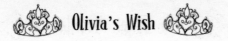

Olivia looked confused. "So, um, who invited you?"

Charlotte and Mia exchanged worried looks. They hadn't been invited to Olivia's party, but they knew they needed to stay. How on earth could they explain it all to Olivia?

"Well, it's, um, kind of hard to explain," said Charlotte, wondering what to say.

"Do ... do you believe in magic?" Mia asked Olivia.

"Of course not!" Olivia said with a laugh. "I mean, I used to when I was little," she said, blushing, "but everyone knows that magic isn't real."

"OK, well, actually ... it is!" said Charlotte. "I know this is going to sound crazy, but Mia and I can do magic."

"We're kind of like fairy godmothers," Mia said, as Olivia's eyes got wider and wider.

"And we're here to use magic to help you," said Charlotte.

"You made a wish, didn't you?" Mia asked her gently.

"Yes," stammered Olivia. "But ... but ..."

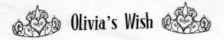

She shook her head. "No, you've got to be joking. Is this a trick?"

"No! We're not," said Mia earnestly.

"Why don't you tell us what your wish is," said Charlotte, seeing how hard Olivia was finding it to believe them. "If we're telling the truth, then hopefully we'll be able to help you. If we're making it up, well, what have you got to lose?"

"OK," said Olivia slowly. "Well, I wished for the best birthday party ever. I thought it might be a way of making new friends. We only moved here last month and I haven't made any friends yet." She looked down at her feet. "I find it really hard to talk to people I don't know."

"Me, too!" Mia told her, nodding her head sympathetically.

"I thought we could have a barbecue and invite a few of the girls from my class at school, but then Mum and Dad hired this party planner, Petra, to organise it all. Now she's taken over and I don't know what she's doing. She keeps saying it's all top secret. All she'll tell me is that it's going to be super stylish ..." Her shoulders dropped and she looked at the girls sadly. "I'm dreading it. What if everyone from school comes and the party is a total disaster?"

"I'm sure it won't be," said Charlotte.

"We'll make sure it's not," said Mia. "But you have to keep who we really are a secret."

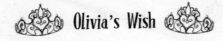

"OK." Olivia shrugged. "It's worth a try!"

"Well, well, well, who have we got here?" A tall, skinny woman in impossibly high heels came into the room. She had a dark green scarf swirled around  her shoulders and was wearing tight leather trousers. She had wavy black hair with an ice-blonde streak at the front, and her nails were very long and painted lime green.

She was very beautiful but she was wearing lots of make-up, and her false eyelashes looked like long, curling spiders' legs.

"These are two of my, er, friends, Petra," said Olivia.

Mia and Charlotte grinned at her gratefully.

"Here early for a sneaky peek, I see!" the party planner said with a high-pitched, sugary laugh. "Well, the tent is ready for you and your little friends to see, Olivia," she told them. Her eyes glittered. "This way!" she trilled. "Come with me!"

They followed her out of the living room and into the next room, a conservatory which had a huge tent attached to it.

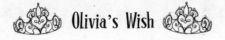

A short covered tunnel ran between the open doors and the tent.

"I hope it looks nice," Olivia whispered to Charlotte and Mia.

"Ta da!" Petra said, opening the tent flap and stepping to one side with a smile that showed a lot of teeth. "What do you think? Isn't it just wonderful?"

"Oh," whispered Olivia faintly.

Charlotte and Mia peered into the tent, then exchanged horrified looks. It looked awful! The inside had been lined with billowing green fabric. The tables were covered with sludge-grey tablecloths. There were big brown vases on each table filled with thorny branches, and the chairs were

made from black twisted metal with spikes
poking up around the edges.

A small, round man with greasy black hair
combed over his scalp was fussing around
the thorny table decorations. Seeing Petra
and the girls, he clasped his hands together
and bowed. "Ah, Meeees Oleeevia," he said,
in a thick accent. "What do you zink of the
amazing, sooper-stylish decorations? Is it not
ze most divine zing you 'av ever seen?"

"Um, well ..." Olivia bit her lip. Her face was pale and Charlotte was sure she was imagining what everyone from her school would say.

"Ah, the little darling is lost for words," smiled Petra. "Mr Hex is my assistant," she told Charlotte and Mia. "He has worked at all the most stylish parties. Now, do come and sample the party food."

She ushered them over to the back of the tent where there was a buffet table laden with silver serving platters and bowls. But all the food on them looked revolting! There were fish heads, crabs' claws and bowls of pale, gloopy mixture that looked like frogspawn. Petra picked up a tray that had a bowl of green slimy dip on, and some strange black biscuits. "Fancy a taste?"

She thrust the tray under Mia's nose.
"Um … OK. Thanks," Mia stuttered.

Once Mia had taken one, Petra passed
the dish to Charlotte. Charlotte didn't like
the look of it at all, but she didn't want to
be rude. She took a biscuit and a tiny bit
of the dip. *Surely it can't taste as bad as it
looks?* she thought. She took a mouthful
and almost choked. It was horrible! It tasted
like mashed-up seaweed! She coughed and
spluttered.

Petra smiled with a slightly spiteful look in
her green eyes. "I suppose you're not used to
such *sophisticated* food. Come along, Hex!"
she called. "We must get Olivia's party
outfit ready."

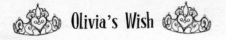

She sailed out of the tent with Hex running after her as fast as his little legs could carry him. Charlotte put the biscuit down on the table. "That's really revolting," she said, pointing at it.

"All the food looks disgusting!" said Olivia. She groaned. "This is going to be the worst party ever. No one is going to want to be my friend after this!" She collapsed into a chair.

and burst into tears, burying her face in her hands.

"Oh, don't cry, Olivia," Mia said, putting an arm around her. "Oh, I wish I could sort the food out for you. I love baking – I could make cupcakes and biscuits … Mum and I even made sausage rolls once."

"But the party's starting in half an hour!" sobbed Oliva. "There isn't time to do anything like that."

A glimmer of light caught Charlotte's eyes. It was coming from Mia's pendant. Glancing down, she saw that her own pendant was glowing too. She gasped and beckoned Mia over to the side of the tent.

"Don't worry, I know how we can change things!" Charlotte whispered.

"How?" asked Mia desperately.

Charlotte grinned. "With wish magic, of course!"

CHAPTER SEVEN
Make a Wish

Charlotte picked up her pendant. It was shining more brightly with every second.

"How do you suppose we make a wish?" she wondered.

"I'm not sure," Mia replied. "But Alice said we need to put our necklaces together."

She and Charlotte brought the two halves of the heart together. As they got closer they

could feel the pendants drawing towards
each other as if they were magnetic. As the
two halves met and formed a perfect heart,
there was a flash of bright light.

"What should we wish for?" said Mia.

"For pretty decorations and nice food,"
said Charlotte.

Mia nodded. "You say it, Charlotte."

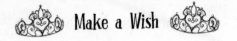

Charlotte took a breath. She really hoped this was going to work. "We wish for the tent to be perfect for Olivia's party!" she exclaimed.

A tingle ran through her fingers and then a stream of sparkles suddenly shot out of the centre of the heart and whizzed around the tent. As sparkles flew across the ceiling, the

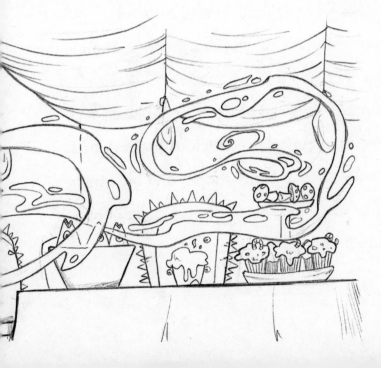

green fabric changed to pale pink silk with pretty patterned bunting looping around the sides of the tent. The sparkles fell on the tables and chairs and they transformed, the spiky black chairs becoming golden with pink heart details and soft pink cushions on the seats, and the tablecloths turning a pure white, with pink napkins.

"Look at the food!" cried Mia, as everything on the buffet table had changed too. The horrible fishy food and bowls of green seaweed gloop were replaced by towers of cupcakes, delicious-looking little sandwiches in heart shapes and big bowls of crisps. There was even a big, wobbly pink jelly!

"Hey, Olivia!" called Charlotte. "Is this more what you had in mind?"

Olivia took her hands away from her face and gazed around the room in astonishment. "This is amazing!" she exclaimed, clapping her hands together in excitement. "You really *are* magic! Thank you! Thank you!" She leaped up and hugged them both.

Charlotte and Mia looked around the tent in delight. It looked so much nicer

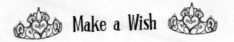

now – just perfect for Olivia's party.

"But what's Petra going to say?" Olivia said, with a gasp.

"Don't worry, the wish magic will fix that," Charlotte said, crossing her fingers behind her back. Alice had said no one would notice the magic, and Charlotte hoped that was true. She didn't know what the party planner would say if she realised that they'd changed everything!

Just then Petra's voice floated out from inside the house. "Olivia! Your dress is ready, darling."

"I'd better go and get changed," said Olivia excitedly. "Will you come and help me get ready?"

"Of course we will," said Mia. "What's your dress like?"

"I don't know," Olivia sighed. "All I know is that Petra had it made by some top designer …"

"It might be nice!" Mia said hopefully.

Leaving the tent, they hurried upstairs. Olivia's room was a lot cosier than the rooms downstairs. There was a bed, a desk, a bookcase and a small sofa with lots of different coloured cushions on. There was a brightly coloured rug on the floor, trinkets on the shelves, and posters of pop stars on the wall, including one of Alice De Silver. Charlotte blinked in surprise as the poster of Alice gave her a wink and a thumbs up!

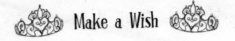
"I like your room!" said Mia.

"Thanks." Olivia smiled. "Mum and Dad always say it's too messy. But I like it."

Petra and Hex popped their heads around the door.

"Knock, knock," said Hex.

"Are you ready to see your outfit?" asked Petra. "I've worked hard to make it perfect."

The party planner and her assistant strode into the room. Petra threw the wardrobe doors open.

"Voila!" the little man cried.

Charlotte and Mia caught their breath in horror.

Inside the wardrobe there was a long mustard-yellow dress

made from a heavy dull
fabric with brown trim
around the sleeves and
neckline. It had a tight
top and a billowing skirt.

"So?" Petra grinned,
flashing her very white
teeth. "What do you
think of your dress?"

Olivia opened and
shut her mouth, not
knowing what to say.

"It's um ... not very ...
me," she said hesitantly.

Petra rolled her eyes.
"Honestly, Olivia!

You clearly have no idea about these kinds of things. It's the latest style. It will be …" She smiled and once again Charlotte thought she saw a spiteful look cross her eyes. "…simply unforgettable." She chuckled. "Now, get changed, dear," she said to Olivia. "Oh, and don't forget to wear these." She strode over to the wardrobe and pulled out a pair of brown, clumpy shoes. "They match the dress perfectly, don't they?"

And with a laugh that sounded suspiciously like a snigger, the party planner strode out of the room.

"I can't wear that dress!" said Olivia, looking aghast. "Everyone will think I'm really weird."

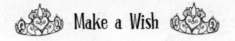

"It's awful," agreed Charlotte.

"What am I going to do?" said Olivia, staring at the dress in dismay.

Mia looked down at her necklace.

Their pendants were still glowing, but more faintly than they had been before the first wish. "It's time for some more magic!"

Charlotte didn't need telling twice. She picked up her pendant and held it to Mia's.

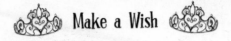

"We wish that Olivia could wear a party dress she really likes," said Mia.

Whoosh!

Sparkles shot out of their necklaces again and swirled around Olivia and the dress. There was a bright flash and suddenly she was standing in front of them dressed in a beautiful, swishy aquamarine dress and pretty matching ballet pumps.

Catching sight of herself in her bedroom mirror, Olivia squealed with delight. "Oh, it's gorgeous!" She twirled around. "It'll be perfect for dancing in! Oh, thank you!"

Charlotte and Mia beamed. "You look lovely!" said Mia.

Just then, the doorbell rang downstairs.

"The guests are arriving!" Olivia said. "Oh, wow! The party's about to begin."

The girls went downstairs. The front door was open and Mr Hex and Petra were showing people inside.

"Hello, hello," Petra trilled to the guests. "So pleased to see you all. Come on in. The party is taking place in a tent at the back.

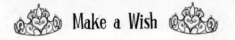

Come right this way!" She and Hex ushered the guests through the hall. They didn't see the girls and Olivia standing on the stairs.

The three girls exchanged looks. Alice had said that nobody but Olivia would notice that they'd used magic, but Charlotte felt a bit nervous, and Mia looked worried too.

Charlotte, Mia and Olivia hovered outside the tent as Petra took the first guests in.

There were lots of oohhs and ahhs as Olivia's school friends went into the pretty tent. Mia and Charlotte exchanged a happy glance. Everyone liked it!

"Ahhhhhhhhhh!" Petra hastily turned her shocked shriek into a coughing fit. *Cough, cough, cough.* "Please excuse me, everyone.

So sorry. I'll go and get a drink of water. Yes, go on in. I'll be back in a moment."

Petra came storming back into the hall. She caught sight of the girls and skidded to a halt. "Your dress!" she gasped, as she caught sight of Olivia's new outfit. "It looks … lovely." Then Petra's green eyes fell on Charlotte's and Mia's necklaces and she stared at them furiously.

Charlotte shivered. She didn't like the way Petra was looking at them. Almost as if she knew what they'd done. But how was that possible? Alice had said that no one would notice the magic …

Before she could say anything, Olivia's mum appeared at the top of the stairs with

a tall man who had the same blue eyes and brown hair as Olivia. He had to be her dad. "Oh, Petra. Is everything ready?" he asked. "It sounds like the guests like it!"

Petra instantly put on a big fake smile. "Yes, they're all gathering in the tent. Why don't you come down and say hello?"

"Great idea," said Olivia's dad.

"Your dress is gorgeous, honey," Olivia's mum said, as she came down the stairs. "You've done a fantastic job, Petra. It's just the sort of thing Olivia loves."

"Yes, she does looks perfectly lovely, doesn't she?" Petra said tightly.

Olivia and her parents headed towards the tent. Charlotte and Mia started to follow when Petra caught them both by the arms.

"Oh, girls, you couldn't do me a massive favour, could you?" she said sweetly. "I need some help in the kitchen." Her bony fingers dug into their arms.

"Well, um, we really wanted to stay with Olivia," Charlotte said, not wanting to be alone with the strange woman.

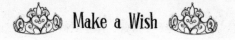

"It'll only take a moment," said Petra. "I'd really appreciate your help."

"OK," Mia said. Petra wasn't very nice, but Mia was always willing to lend a hand – especially if it would make Olivia's party a success.

As Olivia and her parents went into the tent, Petra pushed the girls towards the kitchen. Mr Hex hurried over to Petra. "Are they ... are they ..." he whispered.

"Yes!" Petra hissed. She shoved the girls into the kitchen so forcefully that they both stumbled and almost fell over.

"What are you doing?" gasped Charlotte.

"Keeping you two nuisances out of my way!" snapped Petra. She slammed the

kitchen door and locked it from the other side. "You can stay in here until the party is over!"

CHAPTER EIGHT
Trapped!

Charlotte banged on the door with her fists, but the only sound she heard in reply was Petra and Mr Hex cackling together as they walked off.

"What's going on?" gasped Mia.

"I don't know," said Charlotte. She tugged at the door handle but it wouldn't open. "Let us out!" she called. But the noise from the

party drowned out her cries.

"I don't understand – Alice said no one would notice the magic, but Petra seemed cross. I don't like her at all. I think she *wants* the party to be a disaster. And she was looking at our necklaces really strangely," said Mia anxiously.

"We've got to get out of here," said Charlotte. "Maybe we should use our magic and wish our way out?"

"We can't use wishes for ourselves," Mia reminded her. "We've got to get out another

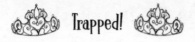

way." She looked around desperately.

"How about we climb out of the window!" said Charlotte suddenly. "It's not that far to the ground."

Mia ran over and looked down nervously. "I don't know. It's a bit high."

"So, let's make a rope," said Charlotte.

Mia's eyes scanned the kitchen. Then she gasped. "I know! We can tie the tea towels together!" she said, pointing at some hanging by the side of the oven.

"Brilliant idea!' said Charlotte.

They grabbed
the tea towels
and knotted them
together. Then
they tied one end
of their makeshift
rope to the leg of
the kitchen table
and dangled the
other end out of the
kitchen window.

Mia watched as
Charlotte swung
over the window
ledge and nimbly
climbed down.

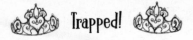

"Your turn," Charlotte called up.

Mia hesitated.

Charlotte looked up at her encouragingly. "Come on, Mia, you can do it," she said. "I'm right here."

Mia climbed down cautiously.

"There you go," Charlotte said, as her friend's feet touched the ground.

"Phew!" said Mia, hugging Charlotte.

"Now, we need to get back into the party," said Charlotte.

They ran to the back garden. But there was a familiar figure at the tent door – Hex!

Luckily Charlotte had an idea. "We can get in this way!" she said, holding up the bottom of the tent and beckoning to Mia.

Mia scrambled under the canvas and
Charlotte followed.

They were just standing up when Olivia
spotted them. "What are you two doing?" she
said, coming over.

"Long story," said Charlotte.

"Is everything OK?" Mia asked anxiously.

"Not really," said Olivia, pulling a face.
"The food and my dress are lovely but the
music's awful. Nobody's having fun."

Very dull classical music was coming
through the speakers. There was no one
on the dance floor and everyone was
just standing around in small huddles,
whispering. It didn't feel like a party at all.

"You can't have a party with this sort of

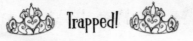

music," Charlotte said, pulling a face.

"I know. I tried to tell Petra that but she wouldn't listen. Apparently this music is—"

"Super stylish?" finished Charlotte. "How did I guess?" She shook her head. "We'll have to do something about it."

"We've only got one wish left to give Olivia a really brilliant party," Mia said.

She picked up her pendant. The glow was faint now. "We'd better make it quickly!"

She held her half-heart pendant out towards Charlotte. As the two halves met and Charlotte took a deep breath. "I wish …"

"I don't think so!" hissed a voice. Their heads jerked up. Petra came striding towards them, with Mr Hex running along behind her. "There's only one person doing magic around here – and that's me!"

Reaching into the top of her dress, she pulled out a necklace with a pendant at the end: a skull and crossbones – the symbol for poison!

She whispered a word and it started to

glow with a sickly green
light. The light spread
over her fingers and
over her whole body.
A second later she
had transformed.

Her ice-blonde
streak now had a
tinge of green and
her scarf and leather
trousers turned into
a slinky, full-length
olive-green gown.
She had a large,
spiky metal tiara
on her head.

She looked beautiful but her lips were cruel and her green eyes were cold as ice. She smiled and brought out a thin black wand with another skull and crossbones on the top.

There was only one person it could be.

"Princess Poison!" Charlotte and Mia gasped.

"Yes!" hissed Princess Poison wickedly.

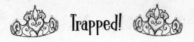
"I'm here to make sure that Olivia's wish
DOESN'T come true!"

Charlotte realised that everything had
gone quiet. She swung round. Everyone else
in the tent had frozen! Some had stopped
mid-chew, others were paused as they talked.
Even Olivia was standing still. Princess
Poison must be using her magic!

Princess Poison saw where they were looking and her lips twisted in a cruel smile. "They'll all stay like that while the three of us have a little chat." Her green eyes raked over Charlotte and Mia. "So, you two are training to become Secret Princesses, are you?" She looked at the half-heart shapes on their necklaces and her face twisted into a sneer. "And a pair of Friendship Princesses, no less. Well, well, well. I imagine you've heard *all* about me." There was a touch of pride to her voice, and she gave a grin that showed a lot of teeth.

"We have," said Charlotte grimly.

"We know that you like to spoil wishes," added Mia.

"Oh, yes, I do." Princess Poison sniggered. "Because it gives me power!" She held her necklace in her hands, her eyes glittering. "Much, much more power than I would ever have as a silly Secret Princess. You two could be powerful too." She pointed at their pendants. "Give that last wish to me and I'll give you something in return. You can join with me and Hex and help us spoil people's wishes."

"Join us!" said Hex, rubbing his hands together. His strange foreign accent had completely disappeared. "We could cause ever so much trouble together."

"We'd never join with you!" cried Charlotte in outrage.

"No way!" said Mia. "We don't want to be mean like you are."

"Well, aren't you two just the most precious little goody-goodies?" said Princess Poison with another sneer. "Think about it, my sweets. With every wish you ruin, your power will grow. Join with me and we will be unstoppable! Imagine being able to use magic to give yourself whatever you want! All your deepest wishes would be granted!" Princess Poison pointed her wand at the girls and a dark green mist snaked out and coiled itself around them.

Charlotte shook her head to clear it. She would never want to spoil anyone's wishes, no matter how much power it gave her.

"So?" demanded Hex greedily. "What do you say?"

Charlotte folded her arms. "I say you should both go away."

"Yes, and stay away," agreed Mia bravely.

"There's no chance of us giving the last wish to you," Charlotte continued. She glanced at Mia. "Anyway, I don't need to steal wishes. My deepest wish has already come true – now that I'm a Secret Princess trainee, I'll get to see Mia lots and lots!"

"Me too," said Mia, taking Charlotte's hand. "There's nothing I want more than to see Charlotte."

"You will both regret this!" Princess Poison's voice sounded like icicles snapping. "Be warned. If you reject my offer, I will do everything in my power from now on to stop you becoming Secret Princesses."

"Oh, really?" Charlotte said defiantly.

"I'd like to see you try!"

Princess Poison lifted her wand high.
A ball of green light exploded from the end
of the wand and shot towards Charlotte.
Charlotte leapt out of the way. Her hands
met the floor and she sprang into a perfect
handspring, just as if she was in one of
her gymnastics classes. The horrid green
light exploded harmlessly behind her.

Mia cheered and whooped.

"Gah!" Princess Poison spat. She swung round and pointed the wand at Mia.

Another green ball of light shot towards Mia. Grabbing a tray off the table, Mia batted the green ball away. It bounced off the tray and shot straight back at Princess Poison.

"No!" the evil princess cried, as the magic hit her. She reeled backwards into Hex.

"Whoa!" he yelled, collapsing into the buffet table. The enormous jelly wobbled wildly and then plopped over the edge and landed on their heads.

"Ew!" shrieked Princess Poison, pulling bits of pink jelly out of her hair.

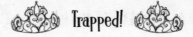

Charlotte and Mia couldn't help it. They started to giggle.

Princess Poison scrambled to her feet. Jelly slithered down her face and onto her shiny dress. "You'll be sorry for this!" she snarled, trembling with rage. "I will make you girls regret the day you turned me down." She grabbed Hex and hauled him to his feet,

slipping and sliding in the jelly. "You'll see me again, mark my words!" Then she clicked her heels together and she and Hex vanished in a cloud of green smoke.

CHAPTER NINE
Party Time!

For a moment the girls just stared at the empty space. "Oh my goodness, I can't believe that just happened!" said Charlotte with a gasp. "Princess Poison was really angry, wasn't she!"

"And scary," said Mia. "I hope we don't meet her again." She looked around, hearing a sudden flood of noise. The guests had all

unfrozen and the boring classical music had
started again.

"Oh, no!" Olivia gasped, looking at the
pools of jelly on the floor. "What happened?"

"There was an accident," said Charlotte,
as she and Mia picked up the tablecloth.
"Someone bumped into the table."

Charlotte and Mia started to clean up the messy jelly.

"Don't worry about that," said Olivia. "I'll find Petra and get her to deal with it." She glanced around. "Where is she?"

"She's gone," said Charlotte truthfully. "One minute she was here, and the next she had disappeared."

"We'll clean this up for you," said Mia helpfully. "Look, it's almost done." She dumped the messy napkins into a bin.

"Thanks. I really wish you could do something about the music too," sighed Olivia sadly.

Charlotte grinned. "Don't forget, your wish is our command! Mia?"

The two of them touched their half-heart pendants together.

"We wish for music that's really good to dance to!" Charlotte said.

There was a bright silver flash and suddenly Alice appeared at the edge of the dance floor! She was wearing her pop-star clothes and had a guitar with her.

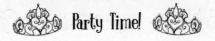

"It's … it's Alice De Silver!" stammered Olivia in excitement.

Charlotte and Mia were just as surprised. They hadn't expected Alice to appear!

All the other guests saw Alice too, and started pointing and gasping.

"Oh my goodness! It's Alice De Silver! Look!" one girl gasped.

Alice winked at Mia and Charlotte and then turned to the audience. "Let's get Olivia's party started!" she whooped. "Come and dance everyone. One, two, three ..." She started to play her guitar and sing. All the guests cheered and raced onto the dance floor.

"I can't believe Alice De Silver is actually here at my birthday party!" said Olivia, looking stunned. "How did you manage it?"

Charlotte and Mia grinned. "Magic, of course!" they said.

"Enough talking. Let's dance!" said Charlotte. She grabbed Olivia and Mia's hands and dragged them both onto the dance floor.

"This is the best party ever!" said one of the girls, dancing nearby.

"I can't believe Alice De Silver is here," said another girl to Olivia.

"It was a surprise for me too," said Olivia. "I love Alice. What's your favourite song?" As they danced they started talking about which songs they liked best.

"Petra really has excelled herself!" Charlotte heard Olivia's mum say. "Who would have guessed she would manage to get Alice De Silver to play here?"

Charlotte hid her grin as she thought of Princess Poison and how furious she would be if she could see how much everyone was enjoying the party.

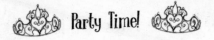

The guests danced and danced until finally Alice took a bow and Olivia's dad led everyone outside. Then Olivia's mum appeared with a big birthday cake. Everyone gathered around the cake while she lit the candles. Then Alice strummed her guitar and struck up the first few notes of 'Happy Birthday'. Soon, everyone was singing along.

Olivia's face was flushed with happiness and her eyes twinkled brightly as she stared around at everyone. "Thank you!" she said when the song had finished.

"This has been the best birthday party ever!"

Suddenly, there was a tinkling sound. The candles on Olivia's birthday cake shot mini fireworks into the air, bursting into dazzling displays of colourful sparkles and showering Olivia and her guests with glitter.

Mia and Charlotte exchanged a grin. Olivia's wish had been granted! Just then, Charlotte and Mia felt a tap on their arms. Alice beckoned them away from the crowd.

"We did it, Alice!" said Charlotte, giving her a big hug.

"Thank you so much for coming," said Mia. "Olivia loved her party."

"And she's made lots of friends tonight," added Charlotte.

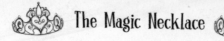

"I was watching you through the mirror in the palace," Alice said. "When I realised that Petra was Princess Poison I was really worried, but you managed brilliantly on your own. You've passed this first task with flying colours. Olivia had a wonderful party." She pulled out a small silver compact. When she opened it, they saw an image of Wishing Star Palace in the mirror. As they watched, a swirl of magic surrounded

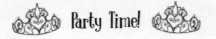

one of the turrets. When it cleared, they could see it looked brand-new. "By stopping Princess Poison you've helped to repair Wishing Star Palace," she said. "But please be extra careful from now on. Princess Poison won't forget this in a hurry."

"We don't care," said Charlotte.

"She's not going to stop us granting wishes," agreed Mia. "We've got each other and together we can do anything!"

Charlotte high-fived her. "Yes! Anything at all!"

Alice's eyes sparkled. "That's exactly why you were both chosen to train as Secret Princesses. Talking of which ..." She gently touched her wand to Charlotte's necklace.

Charlotte gasped as a sparkling diamond suddenly appeared on the half-heart pendant. Then Alice did the same to Mia.

"You granted Olivia's wish, so you've earned your first diamond," Alice told them. "You're one step closer to earning your tiaras. Now, say goodbye to each other and I'll use my magic to send you both home."

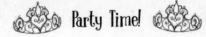

Charlotte and Mia
flung their arms
around each other
and hugged tightly.

"It's been so good
to see you," said
Charlotte. "I've
missed you so much."

"Me too," Mia
told her. "But we
don't need to miss
each other any more,
because we'll meet again soon at Wishing
Star Palace."

"And grant some more wishes," Charlotte
said determinedly.

"Even if sneaky Princess Poison tries to stop us!" declared Mia.

They hugged one more time and then sparkles rushed out of Alice's wand and Charlotte felt herself whizzing away.

She landed back in her sunny bedroom in California. It was so strange to be back. So much had happened and yet to the rest of her family it would seem as if she hadn't been away at all.

She sank down on her bed. Next to her schoolbag was an invitation to the school dance. Charlotte looked at it thoughtfully. Maybe she would go to the dance after all. Leah and Ava had sounded like they really wanted her to come when they'd invited her,

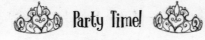

and dancing was the perfect way to make
new friends – Olivia's party had shown her
that. *I'll go,* she thought to herself.

Charlotte suddenly realised that the ache
in her heart from missing Mia had faded,
and instead she was full of excitement.
Touching the diamond on her necklace,
she smiled happily. They'd got one diamond,

and now they only had to get three more
before they got their proper princess tiaras.
It was just the beginning – there were lots
more Secret Princess adventures to come!

The End

Join Charlotte and Mia in their next Secret Princesses adventure!

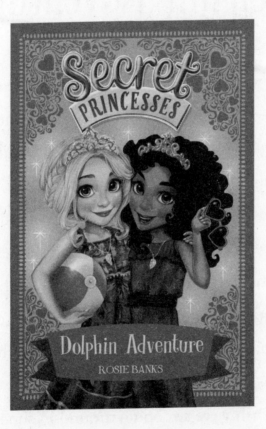

Read on for a sneak peek!

Dolphin Adventure

"This way, please!" the tour guide called, leading the class through the dark tunnels of the aquarium. "In here you'll see a wonderful display of tropical fish."

Mia Thompson tucked her long blonde hair behind her ears and followed the rest of her class into the next room. One wall had a large pane of glass that reached from the floor all the way up to the ceiling. On the other side of the glass, tiny blue, yellow and green fish were swooping around in shoals while larger orange fish weaved between all the rocks and seaweed.

"So, who can tell me what fish eat?" the guide asked.

"Fish food!" one of the boys called out.

Everyone giggled.

The guide smiled. "Well, yes, but what is fish food in the wild?"

Mia knew the answer was plankton – she knew lots of facts about animals and sea creatures – but she was too shy to put up her hand.

"The little fish eat plankton," said the guide, when no one else answered. "Plankton are tiny creatures that float in the water."

Mia went closer to the glass. For a moment, she imagined being a mermaid, swimming among all the wonderful fish. She half turned to tell her best friend, Charlotte, what she was thinking, before she realised that Charlotte wasn't there. Charlotte had moved to America with her family a few weeks ago. Mia felt a pang of sadness in her heart. She and Charlotte had been best friends since they were little and they had always done everything together.

We still get to do some things together, though! she thought. Touching the golden necklace that was hidden under her school jumper, Mia smiled as she thought of the incredible secret she and Charlotte shared. Hanging on each necklace was a pendant in the shape of half a heart. They had been given to the girls by their grown-up friend, Alice, who used to be their neighbour. When Charlotte had moved away, the girls had both wished to see each other – and something absolutely amazing had happened. The necklaces had whisked both girls away to a gorgeous palace that floated high up in the clouds! Alice had met them there and told them she was a Secret Princess – someone who could magically grant wishes. Mia and Charlotte had been even more astonished when Alice had told them that they had the potential to become Secret Princesses, too!

Suddenly, Mia felt a tingle run across her skin. Her necklace! Dropping away from her class as they followed the guide towards the next display, she slipped back into the tunnel and pulled the necklace out.

Warm light sparkled off it, lighting up the dim tunnel. Mia's heart skipped a beat. If her necklace was glowing, it meant she was going to see Charlotte. Maybe they'd even get to grant another wish!

She closed her fingers around the pendant. *I wish I could see Charlotte,* she thought. The world seemed to drop away and she was spinning and tumbling through the air. Luckily no time passed in their real lives while she and Charlotte were away on a Secret Princess adventure, so no one would even notice she was gone.

Mia's feet hit soft grass and her eyes
blinked open. She was standing in a
beautiful garden filled with rose bushes,
and her school clothes had changed into
a gorgeous golden dress with a floaty skirt.
She put her hand up and felt a tiara nestling
in her blonde hair. Wisps of fluffy white
cloud were floating around the garden,
and lollipops and candyfloss hung from the
branches of the trees. Mia ran to an archway
of roses and looked through.

"Wishing Star Palace!" she breathed
in excitement as she saw the grand white
palace with its four turrets twisting up into
the sky. It looked beautiful from a distance,
but Mia knew that if she got closer she would

see that the paint was peeling, there were tiles missing from the turrets and that the panes of glass in the heart-shaped windows were cracked. She and Charlotte were determined to make it beautiful again!

"Mia! Mia!"

Swinging round, Mia saw Charlotte running towards her, her brown curls bouncing on her shoulders and a delighted smile on her freckly face. She was wearing a light pink princess dress with roses on the skirt, and like Mia she had her pendant around her neck and a golden tiara in her hair.

With a squeal of joy, Mia raced towards her best friend and they hugged each other.

"Oh wow! I can't believe we're back!" said Charlotte, letting go of Mia and jumping up and down with excitement. "I almost thought I'd dreamt it."

"We didn't dream it," said Mia, looking at the half-heart pendant. "The diamond proves it really happened!"

When Alice had first given them their necklaces, the half-hearts had been pure gold, but after they granted a girl named Olivia's wish to have a brilliant birthday party, a diamond had appeared in each of their pendants. Alice had explained that if they helped three more people, they'd get three more diamonds. Once they had them all, their plain tiaras would turn into the beautiful jewelled tiaras that all Secret Princesses wore. Even more importantly, they would be one step closer to becoming fully fledged Secret Princesses!

"Should we go to the palace and see if we can find Alice?" asked Mia, excitement bubbling through her.

Holding hands, they ran through the arch. As they got closer to the palace, Charlotte pointed upwards. Three of the turrets had missing tiles, but one of the turrets looked like new, its golden tiles glittering in the sunshine.

"Look!" said Charlotte. "It's the turret that got mended when we made Olivia's wish come true."

Mia nodded proudly. "I hope we can repair more of Wishing Star Palace by granting someone else's wish."

"I bet we will," said Charlotte. "Oh, I can't wait to have another adventure!"

Read *Dolphin Adventure* to find out what happens next!

CHARLOTTE

In the real world
Charlotte lives in California, USA with her parents and six-year-old twin brothers, Liam and Harvey.

Personality
Bubbly, confident and funny – Charlotte loves telling jokes!

Hobbies
Playing sports, doing gymnastics and dancing.

Favourite colour
Pale pink.

Symbol on her necklace
Half a heart. It matches her best friend Mia's pendant, showing that they are both training to become Friendship Princesses.

Favourite thing about Wishing Star Palace
The gorgeous gardens to run around in.

MIA

In the real world
Mia lives with her parents and
little sister, Elsie, in the UK.
They have a pet cat named Flossie.

Personality
Shy, kind and creative.

Hobbies
Baking tasty treats and
doing crafts.

Favourite colour
Turquoise blue.

Symbol on her necklace
Half a heart. It matches her best
friend Charlotte's pendant,
showing that they are both training
to become Friendship Princesses.

Favourite thing about Wishing Star Palace
The animals Princess Ella looks after.

PRINCESS ALICE

In the real world
Princess Alice is the pop star Alice De Silver. Before she became famous she was Mia and Charlotte's babysitter.

Personality
Warm, friendly and glamorous.

Hobbies
Singing and playing the guitar.

Favourite colour
Ruby red.

Symbol on her necklace
A musical note.

Favourite thing about Wishing Star Palace
Getting inspired by her Secret Princess friends.

PRINCESS POISON

In the real world
Princess Poison is an
actress, which is why
she is very good at
disguising herself.

Personality
Bitter, cruel and nasty.

Hobbies
Ruining wishes and shouting
at her servant, Hex.

Favourite colour
Dark green.

Symbol on her necklace
A skull and crossbones.

Favourite thing about
Wishing Star Palace
Nothing at all! She was
banished from the palace
after turning bad.

♥ WIN A PRINCESS OUTFIT ♥

What would you wish for?

Win a Secret Princess outfit
for you and your best friend!

On the cover of this book, Charlotte and Mia
are wearing beautiful outfits designed by

MONSOON

CHILDREN

For a chance to win a magical outfit for you
and another for your very best friend,
just enter our competition by going to

uk.monsoon.co.uk/secret-princesses

Closing date 31st October 2016.
Please see the website above for full terms and conditions.

♡ # FREE NECKLACE ♡

In every book of Secret Princesses series one: The Diamond Collection, there is a special Wish Token. Collect all four tokens to get an exclusive Best Friends necklace by

MONSOON

CHILDREN

for you and your best friend!

Simply fill in the form below, send it in with your four tokens and we'll send you your special necklaces.*

Send to: Secret Princesses Wish Token Offer, Hachette Children's Books Marketing Department, Carmelite House, 50 Victoria Embankment, London, EC4Y 0DZ

Closing Date: 31st December 2016

secretprincessesbooks.co.uk

✄

se complete using capital letters (UK and Republic of Ireland
ents only)

T NAME:

NAME:

E OF BIRTH: DD | MM | YYYY

RESS LINE 1:

RESS LINE 2:

RESS LINE 3:

CODE:

NT OR GUARDIAN'S EMAIL ADDRESS:

like to receive regular Secret Princesses email newsletters and information about
er great Hachette Children's Group offers (I can unsubscribe at any time).

like to receive regular Monsoon Children email newsletters
can unsubscribe at any time).

Terms and Conditions apply. For full terms and conditions please go to
secretprincessesbooks.co.uk/terms

1 Secret Princesses Wish Token

* 2000 necklace available while stocks last.
Terms and conditions apply.

Secret PRINCESSES

What would you wish for?

Are you a Secret Princess?

Join the Secret Princesses Club at:

secretprincessesbooks.co.uk

Explore the magic of the
Secret Princesses and discover:

♥ Special competitions! ♥
♥ Exclusive content! ♥
♥ All the latest princess news! ♥

Open to UK and Republic of Ireland residents only
Please ask your parent/guardian for their permission to join

For full terms and conditions go to
secretprincessesbooks.co.uk/terms